'HIS HA
SOUG
ADJAC
AND SORROW
PARALLELED DESIRE
IN THE IMMENSE
COMPLEXITY
OF LOVE.'

CARSON MCCULLERS

Born 1917, Columbus, Georgia, USA
Died 1967, Nyack, New York, USA

*The Sojourner* was first published in *Mademoiselle* in 1950 and *A Domestic Dilemma* was first published in the *New York Post* magazine section in 1951; both appeared in *The Ballad of the Sad Café* in 1951. *The Haunted Boy* was first published in *Mademoiselle* in 1955 and was posthumously published, amongst other stories, in *The Mortgaged Heart* in 1972.

MCCULLERS IN PENGUIN MODERN CLASSICS

*The Ballad of the Sad Café*
*Clock Without Hands*
*The Heart is a Lonely Hunter*
*The Member of the Wedding*
*The Mortgaged Heart*
*Reflections in a Golden Eye*
*Wunderkind*

CARSON MCCULLERS

# *The Haunted Boy*

PENGUIN BOOKS

PENGUIN CLASSICS

UK | USA | Canada | Ireland | Australia
India | New Zealand | South Africa

Penguin Books is part of the Penguin Random House group
of companies whose addresses can be found at
global.penguinrandomhouse.com.

This selection first published 2018
001



Set in 11.2/13.75 pt Dante MT Std
Typeset by Jouve (UK), Milton Keynes
Printed in Great Britain by Clays Ltd, St Ives plc

ISBN: 978–0–241–33950–3

# *Contents*

## *The Haunted Boy*

Hugh looked for his mother at the corner, but she was not in the yard. Sometimes she would be out fooling with the border of spring flowers – the candytuft, the sweet William, the lobelias (she had taught him the names) – but today the green front lawn with the borders of many-colored flowers was empty under the frail sunshine of the mid-April afternoon. Hugh raced up the sidewalk, and John followed him. They finished the front steps with two bounds, and the door slammed after them.

'Mamma!' Hugh called.

It was then, in the unanswering silence as they stood in the empty, wax-floored hall, that Hugh felt there was something wrong. There was no fire in the grate of the sitting room, and since he was used to the flicker of fire-light during the cold months, the room on this first warm day seemed strangely naked and cheerless. Hugh shivered. He was glad John was there. The sun shone on a red piece in the flowered rug. Redbright, red-dark, red-dead – Hugh sickened with a sudden chill remembrance of 'the other time'. The red darkened to a dizzy black.

'What's the matter, Brown?' John asked. 'You look so white.'

Hugh shook himself and put his hand to his forehead. 'Nothing. Let's go back to the kitchen.'

'I can't stay but just a minute,' John said. 'I'm obligated to sell those tickets. I have to eat and run.'

The kitchen, with the fresh checked towels and clean pans, was now the best room in the house. And on the enameled table there was a lemon pie that she had made. Assured by the everyday kitchen and the pie, Hugh stepped back into the hall and raised his face again to call upstairs.

'Mother! Oh, Mamma!'

Again there was no answer.

'My mother made this pie,' he said. Quickly, he found a knife and cut into the pie – to dispel the gathering sense of dread.

'Think you ought to cut it, Brown?'

'Sure thing, Laney.'

They called each other by their last names this spring, unless they happened to forget. To Hugh it seemed sporty and grown and somehow grand. Hugh liked John better than any other boy at school. John was two years older than Hugh, and compared to him the other boys seemed like a silly crowd of punks. John was the best student in the sophomore class, brainy but not the least bit a teacher's pet, and he was the best athlete too. Hugh was a freshman and didn't have so many friends that first year of high school – he had somehow cut himself off, because he was so afraid.

'Mamma always has me something nice for after school.' Hugh put a big piece of pie on a saucer for John – for Laney.

'This pie is certainly super.'

'The crust is made of crunched-up graham crackers instead of regular pie dough,' Hugh said, 'because pie dough is a lot of trouble. We think this graham-cracker pastry is just as good. Naturally, my mother can make regular pie dough if she wants to.'

Hugh could not keep still; he walked up and down the kitchen, eating the pie wedge he carried on the palm of his hand. His brown hair was mussed with nervous rakings, and his gentle gold-brown eyes were haunted with pained perplexity. John, who remained seated at the table, sensed Hugh's uneasiness and wrapped one gangling leg around the other.

'I'm really obligated to sell those Glee Club tickets.'

'Don't go. You have the whole afternoon.' He was afraid of the empty house. He needed John, he needed someone; most of all he needed to hear his mother's voice and know she was in the house with him. 'Maybe Mamma is taking a bath,' he said. 'I'll holler again.'

The answer to his third call too was silence.

'I guess your mother must have gone to the movie or gone shopping or something.'

'No,' Hugh said. 'She would have left a note. She always does when she's gone when I come home from school.'

'We haven't looked for a note,' John said. 'Maybe she left it under the doormat or somewhere in the living room.'

Hugh was inconsolable. 'No. She would have left it right under this pie. She knows I always run first to the kitchen.'

'Maybe she had a phone call or thought of something she suddenly wanted to do.'

'She *might* have,' he said. 'I remember she said to Daddy that one of these days she was going to buy herself some new clothes.' This flash of hope did not survive its expression. He pushed his hair back and started from the room. 'I guess I'd better go upstairs. I ought to go upstairs while you are here.'

He stood with his arm around the newel post; the smell of varnished stairs, the sight of the closed white bathroom door at the top revived again 'the other time.'

He clung to the newel post, and his feet would not move to climb the stairs. The red turned again to whirling, sick dark. Hugh sat down. *Stick your head between your legs*, he ordered, remembering Scout first aid.

'Hugh,' John called. 'Hugh!'

The dizziness clearing, Hugh accepted a fresh chagrin – Laney was calling him by his ordinary first name; he thought he was a sissy about his mother, unworthy of being called by his last name in the grand, sporty way they used before. The dizziness cleared when he returned to the kitchen.

'Brown,' said John, and the chagrin disappeared. 'Does this establishment have anything pertaining to a cow? A white, fluid liquid. In French they call it *lait*. Here we call it plain old milk.'

The stupidity of shock lightened. 'Oh, Laney, I am a dope! Please excuse me. I clean forgot.' Hugh fetched the milk from the refrigerator and found two glasses. 'I didn't think. My mind was on something else.'

'I know,' John said. After a moment he asked in a calm voice, looking steadily at Hugh's eyes: 'Why are you so worried about your mother? Is she sick, Hugh?'

Hugh knew now that the first name was not a slight; it was because John was talking too serious to be sporty. He liked John better than any friend he had ever had. He felt more natural sitting across the kitchen table from

John, somehow safer. As he looked into John's gray, peaceful eyes, the balm of affection soothed the dread.

John asked again, still steadily: 'Hugh, is your mother sick?'

Hugh could have answered no other boy. He had talked with no one about his mother, except his father, and even those intimacies had been rare, oblique. They could approach the subject only when they were occupied with something else, doing carpentry work or the two times they hunted in the woods together – or when they were cooking supper or washing dishes.

'She's not exactly sick,' he said, 'but Daddy and I have been worried about her. At least, we used to be worried for a while.'

John asked: 'Is it a kind of heart trouble?'

Hugh's voice was strained. 'Did you hear about that fight I had with that slob Clem Roberts? I scraped his slob face on the gravel walk and nearly killed him sure enough. He's still got scars or at least he did have a bandage on for two days. I had to stay in school every afternoon for a week. But I nearly killed him. I would have if Mr Paxton hadn't come along and dragged me off.'

'I heard about it.'

'You know why I wanted to kill him?'

For a moment John's eyes flickered away.

Hugh tensed himself; his raw boy hands clutched the table edge; he took a deep, hoarse breath. 'That slob was telling everybody that my mother was in Milledgeville. He was spreading it around that my mother was crazy.'

'The dirty . . .'

Hugh said in a clear, defeated voice, 'My mother *was* in Milledgeville. But that doesn't mean that she was crazy,' he added quickly. 'In that big State hospital, there are buildings for people who are crazy, and there are other buildings, for people who are just sick. Mamma was sick for a while. Daddy and me discussed it and decided that the hospital in Milledgeville was the place where there were the best doctors and she would get the best care. But she was the furtherest from crazy than anybody in the world. You know Mamma, John.' He said again, 'I ought to go upstairs.'

John said: 'I have always thought that your mother is one of the nicest ladies in this town.'

'You see, Mamma had a peculiar thing happen, and afterward she was blue.'

Confession, the first deep-rooted words, opened the festered secrecy of the boy's heart, and he continued more rapidly, urgent and finding unforeseen relief.

'Last year my mother thought she was going to have a little baby. She talked it over with Daddy and me,' he said proudly. 'We wanted a girl. I was going to choose the name. We were so tickled. I hunted up all my old toys – my electric train and the tracks . . . I was going to name her Crystal – how does the name strike you for a girl? It reminds me of something bright and dainty.'

'Was the little baby born dead?'

Even with John, Hugh's ears turned hot; his cold hands touched them. 'No, it was what they call a tumor. That's what happened to my mother. They had to operate at the hospital here.' He was embarrassed and his voice was very low. 'Then she had something called change of life.' The words were terrible to Hugh. 'And afterward she was blue. Daddy said it was a shock to her nervous system. It's something that happens to ladies; she was just blue and rundown.'

Although there was no red, no red in the kitchen anywhere, Hugh was approaching 'the other time.'

'One day, she just sort of gave up – one day last fall.' Hugh's eyes were wide open and glaring: again he climbed the stairs and opened the bathroom door – he put his hand to his eyes to shut out the memory. 'She tried to – hurt herself. I found her when I came in from school.'

John reached out and carefully stroked Hugh's sweatered arm.

'Don't worry. A lot of people have to go to hospitals because they are rundown and blue. Could happen to anybody.'

'We had to put her in the hospital – the best hospital.' The recollection of those long, long months was stained with a dull loneliness, as cruel in its lasting unappeasement as 'the other time' – how long had it lasted? In the hospital Mamma could walk around and she always had on shoes.

John said carefully: 'This pie is certainly super.'

'My mother is a super cook. She cooks things like meat pie and salmon loaf – as well as steaks and hot dogs.'

'I hate to eat and run,' John said.

Hugh was so frightened of being left alone that he felt the alarm in his own loud heart.

'Don't go,' he urged. 'Let's talk for a little while.'

'Talk about what?'

Hugh could not tell him. Not even John Laney. He could tell no one of the empty house and the horror of the time before. 'Do you ever cry?' he asked John. 'I don't'

'I do sometimes,' John admitted.

'I wish I had known you better when Mother was away. Daddy and me used to go hunting nearly every Saturday. We *lived* on quail and dove. I bet you would have liked that.' He added in a lower tone, 'On Sunday we went to the hospital.'

John said: 'It's a kind of a delicate proposition selling those tickets. A lot of people don't enjoy the High School

Glee Club operettas. Unless they know someone in it personally, they'd rather stay home with a good TV show. A lot of people buy tickets on the basis of being public-spirited.'

'We're going to get a television set real soon.'

'I couldn't exist without television,' John said.

Hugh's voice was apologetic. 'Daddy wants to clean up the hospital bills first because as everybody knows sickness is a very expensive proposition. Then we'll get TV.'

John lifted his milk glass. 'Skoal,' he said. 'That's a Swedish word you say before you drink. A good-luck word.'

'You know so many foreign words and languages.'

'Not so many,' John said truthfully. 'Just *kaput* and *adios* and *skoal* and stuff we learn in French class. That's not much.'

'That's *beaucoup*,' said Hugh, and he felt witty and pleased with himself.

Suddenly the stored tension burst into physical activity. Hugh grabbed the basketball out on the porch and rushed into the backyard. He dribbled the ball several times and aimed at the goal his father had put up on his last birthday. When he missed he bounced the ball to John, who had come after him. It was good to be outdoors and the relief of natural play brought Hugh the first line of a poem. 'My heart is like a basketball.'

Usually when a poem came to him he would lie sprawled on the living-room floor, studying to hunt rhymes, his tongue working on the side of his mouth. His mother would call him Shelley-Poe when she stepped over him, and sometimes she would put her foot lightly on his behind. His mother always liked his poems; today the second line came quickly, like magic. He said it out loud to John: '"My heart is like a basketball, bouncing with glee down the hall." How do you like that for the start of a poem?'

'Sounds kind of crazy to me,' John said. Then he corrected himself hastily. 'I mean it sounds – odd. Odd, I meant.'

Hugh realized why John had changed the word, and the elation of play and poems left him instantly. He caught the ball and stood with it cradled in his arms. The afternoon was golden and the wisteria vine on the porch was in full, unshattered bloom. The wisteria was like lavender waterfalls. The fresh breeze smelled of sun-warmed flowers. The sunlit sky was blue and cloudless. It was the first warm day of spring.

'I have to shove off,' John said.

'No!' Hugh's voice was desperate. 'Don't you want another piece of pie? I never heard of anybody eating just one piece of pie.'

He steered John into the house and this time he called

only out of habit because he always called on coming in. 'Mother!' He was cold after the bright, sunny outdoors. He was cold not only because of the weather but because he was so scared.

'My mother has been home a month and every afternoon she's always here when I come home from school. Always, always.'

They stood in the kitchen looking at the lemon pie. And to Hugh the cut pie looked somehow – odd. As they stood motionless in the kitchen the silence was creepy and odd too.

'Doesn't this house seem quiet to you?'

'It's because you don't have television. We put on our TV at seven o'clock and it stays on all day and night until we go to bed. Whether anybody's in the living room or not. There're plays and skits and gags going on continually.'

'We have a radio, of course, and a vic.'

'But that's not the company of a good TV. You won't know when your mother is in the house or not when you get TV.'

Hugh didn't answer. Their footsteps sounded hollow in the hall. He felt sick as he stood on the first step with his arm around the newel post. 'If you could just come upstairs for a minute —'

John's voice was suddenly impatient and loud. 'How

many times have I told you I'm obligated to sell those tickets. You have to be public-spirited about things like Glee Clubs.'

'Just for a second – I have something important to show you upstairs.'

John did not ask what it was and Hugh sought desperately to name something important enough to get John upstairs. He said finally: 'I'm assembling a hi-fi machine. You have to know a lot about electronics – my father is helping me.'

But even when he spoke he knew John did not for a second believe the lie. Who would buy a hi-fi when they didn't have television? He hated John, as you hate people you have to need so badly. He had to say something more and he straightened his shoulders.

'I just want you to know how much I value your friendship. During these past months I had somehow cut myself off from people.'

'That's OK, Brown. You oughtn't to be so sensitive because your mother was – where she was.'

John had his hand on the door and Hugh was trembling. 'I thought if you could come up for just a minute —'

John looked at him with anxious, puzzled eyes. Then he asked slowly: 'Is there something you are scared of upstairs?'

Hugh wanted to tell him everything. But he could not

tell what his mother had done that September afternoon. It was too terrible and – odd. It was like something a *patient* would do, and not like his mother at all. Although his eyes were wild with terror and his body trembled, he said: 'I'm not scared.'

'Well, so long. I'm sorry I have to go – but to be obligated is to be obligated.'

John closed the front door, and he was alone in the empty house. Nothing could save him now. Even if a whole crowd of boys were listening to TV in the living room, laughing at funny gags and jokes, it would still not help him. He had to go upstairs and find her. He sought courage from the last thing John had said, and repeated the words aloud: 'To be obligated is to be obligated.' But the words did not give him any of John's thoughtlessness and courage; they were creepy and strange in the silence.

He turned slowly to go upstairs. His heart was not like a basketball but like a fast, jazz drum, beating faster and faster as he climbed the stairs. His feet dragged as though he waded through knee-deep water and he held on to the banisters. The house looked odd, crazy. As he looked down at the ground-floor table with the vase of fresh spring flowers that too looked somehow peculiar. There was a mirror on the second floor and his own face startled him, so crazy did it seem to him. The initial of his high-school sweater was backward and wrong in the reflection and his mouth was open like an asylum idiot. He shut his mouth and he looked better. Still the objects he saw – the table downstairs, the sofa upstairs – looked somehow cracked or jarred because of the dread in him, although they were the familiar things of everyday. He fastened his eyes on the closed door at the right of the stairs and the fast, jazz drum beat faster.

He opened the bathroom door and for a moment the dread that had haunted him all that afternoon made him see again the room as he had seen it 'the other time'. His mother lay on the floor and there was blood everywhere. His mother lay there dead and there was blood everywhere, on her slashed wrist, and a pool of blood had trickled to the bathtub and lay dammed there. Hugh touched the doorframe and steadied himself. Then the room settled and he realized this was not 'the other time'. The April sunlight brightened the clean white tiles. There was only bathroom brightness and the sunny window. He went to the bedroom and saw the empty bed with the rose-colored spread. The lady things were on the dresser. The room was as it always looked and nothing had happened . . . nothing had happened and he flung himself on the quilted rose bed and cried from relief and a strained, bleak tiredness that had lasted so long. The sobs jerked his whole body and quieted his jazz, fast heart.

Hugh had not cried all those months. He had not cried at 'the other time', when he found his mother alone in that empty house with blood everywhere. He had not cried but he made a Scout mistake. He had first lifted his mother's heavy, bloody body before he tried to bandage her. He had not cried when he called his father. He had not cried those few days when they were deciding what to do. He hadn't even cried when the doctor suggested Milledgeville, or when he and his father took her to the hospital in the car – although his father cried on the way home. He had not cried at the meals they made – steak every night for a whole month so that they felt steak was running out of their eyes, their ears; then they had switched to hot dogs, and ate them until hot dogs ran out of their ears, their eyes. They got in ruts of food and were messy about the kitchen, so that it was never nice except the Saturday the cleaning woman came. He did not cry those lonesome afternoons after he had the fight with Clem Roberts and felt the other boys were thinking queer things of his mother. He stayed at home in the messy kitchen, eating fig newtons or chocolate bars. Or he went to see a neighbor's television – Miss Richards, an old maid who saw old-maid shows. He had not cried when his father drank too much so that it took his appetite and Hugh had to eat alone. He had not even cried on those long, waiting Sundays when they went to

Milledgeville and he twice saw a lady on a porch without any shoes on and talking to herself. A lady who was a patient and who struck at him with a horror he could not name. He did not cry when at first his mother would say: *Don't punish me by making me stay here. Let me go home.* He had not cried at the terrible words that haunted him – 'change of life' – 'crazy' – 'Milledgeville' – he could not cry all during those long months strained with dullness and want and dread.

He still sobbed on the rose bedspread which was soft and cool against his wet cheeks. He was sobbing so loud that he did not hear the front door open, did not even hear his mother call or the footsteps on the stairs. He still sobbed when his mother touched him and burrowed his face hard in the spread. He even stiffened his legs and kicked his feet.

'Why, Loveyboy,' his mother said, calling him a long-ago child name. 'What's happened?'

He sobbed even louder, although his mother tried to turn his face to her. He wanted her to worry. He did not turn around until she had finally left the bed, and then he looked at her. She had on a different dress – blue silk it looked like in the pale spring light.

'Darling, what's happened?'

The terror of the afternoon was over, but he could not

tell it to his mother. He could not tell her what he had feared, or explain the horror of things that were never there at all – but had once been there.

'Why did you do it?'

'The first warm day I just suddenly decided to buy myself some new clothes.'

But he was not talking about clothes; he was thinking about 'the other time' and the grudge that had started when he saw the blood and horror and felt *why did she do this to me.* He thought of the grudge against the mother he loved the most in the world. All those last, sad months the anger had bounced against the love with guilt between.

'I bought two dresses and two petticoats. How do you like them?'

'I hate them!' Hugh said angrily. 'Your slip is showing.'

She turned around twice and the petticoat showed terribly. 'It's supposed to show, goofy. It's the style.'

'I still don't like it.'

'I ate a sandwich at the tearoom with two cups of cocoa and then went to Mendel's. There were so many pretty things I couldn't seem to get away. I bought these two dresses and look, Hugh! The shoes!'

His mother went to the bed and switched on the light so he could see. The shoes were flat-heeled and *blue* – with diamond sparkles on the toes. He did not know how to criticize. 'They look more like evening shoes than things you wear on the street.'

'I have never owned any colored shoes before. I couldn't resist them.'

His mother sort of danced over toward the window, making the petticoat twirl under the new dress. Hugh had stopped crying now, but he was still angry.

'I don't like it because it makes you look like you're trying to seem young, and I bet you are forty years old.'

His mother stopped dancing and stood still at the window. Her face was suddenly quiet and sad. 'I'll be forty-three years old in June.'

He had hurt her and suddenly the anger vanished and there was only love. 'Mamma, I shouldn't have said that.'

'I realized when I was shopping that I hadn't been in a store for more than a year. Imagine!'

Hugh could not stand the sad quietness and the mother he loved so much. He could not stand his love or his mother's prettiness. He wiped the tears on the sleeve of his sweater and got up from the bed. 'I have never seen you so pretty, or a dress and slip so pretty.' He crouched down before his mother and touched the bright shoes. 'The shoes are really super.'

'I thought the minute I laid eyes on them that you would like them.' She pulled Hugh up and kissed him on the cheek. 'Now I've got lipstick on you.'

Hugh quoted a witty remark he had heard before as he scrubbed off the lipstick. 'It only shows I'm popular.'

'Hugh, why were you crying when I came in? Did something at school upset you?'

'It was only that when I came in and found you gone and no note or anything —'

'I forgot all about a note.'

'And all afternoon I felt – John Laney came in but he had to go sell Glee Club tickets. All afternoon I felt —'

'What? What was the matter?'

But he could not tell the mother he loved about the terror and the cause. He said at last: 'All afternoon I felt – odd.'

Afterward when his father came home he called Hugh to come out into the backyard with him. His father had a worried look – as though he spied a valuable tool Hugh had left outside. But there was no tool and the basketball was put back in its place on the back porch.

'Son,' his father said, 'there's something I want to tell you.'

'Yes, sir?'

'Your mother said that you had been crying this afternoon.' His father did not wait for him to explain. 'I just want us to have a close understanding with each other. Is there anything about school – or girls – or something that puzzles you? Why were you crying?'

Hugh looked back at the afternoon and already it was far away, distant as a peculiar view seen at the wrong end of a telescope.

'I don't know,' he said. 'I guess maybe I was somehow nervous.'

His father put his arm around his shoulder. 'Nobody can be nervous before they are sixteen years old. You have a long way to go.'

'I know.'

'I have never seen your mother look so well. She looks so gay and pretty, better than she's looked in years. Don't you realize that?'

'The slip – the petticoat is supposed to show. It's a new style.'

'Soon it will be summer,' his father said. 'And we'll go on picnics – the three of us.' The words brought an instant vision of glare on the yellow creek and the summer-leaved, adventurous woods. His father added: 'I came out here to tell you something else.'

'Yes, sir?'

'I just want you to know that I realize how fine you were all that bad time. How fine, how damn fine.'

His father was using a swear word as if he were talking to a grown man. His father was not a person to hand out compliments – always he was strict with report cards and tools left around. His father never praised him or used grown words or anything. Hugh felt his face grow hot and he touched it with his cold hands.

'I just wanted to tell you that, son.' He shook Hugh by the shoulder. 'You'll be taller than your old man in a year or so.' Quickly his father went into the house, leaving Hugh to the sweet and unaccustomed aftermath of praise.

Hugh stood in the darkening yard after the sunset colors faded in the west and the wisteria was dark purple. The kitchen light was on and he saw his mother fixing dinner. He knew that something was finished; the terror was far from him now, also the anger that had bounced with love, the dread and guilt. Although he felt he would never cry again – or at least not until he was sixteen – in the brightness of his tears glistened the safe, lighted kitchen, now that he was no longer a haunted boy, now that he was glad somehow, and not afraid.

# *The Sojourner*

The twilight border between sleep and waking was a Roman one this morning: splashing fountains and arched, narrow streets, the golden lavish city of blossoms and age-soft stone. Sometimes in this semi-consciousness he sojourned again in Paris, or war German rubble, or Swiss ski-ing and a snow hotel. Sometimes, also, in a fallow Georgia field at hunting dawn. Rome it was this morning in the yearless region of dreams.

John Ferris awoke in a room in a New York hotel. He had the feeling that something unpleasant was awaiting him – what it was, he did not know. The feeling, submerged by matinal necessities, lingered even after he had dressed and gone downstairs. It was a cloudless autumn day and the pale sunlight sliced between the pastel skyscrapers. Ferris went into the next-door drugstore and sat at the end booth next to the window glass that overlooked the sidewalk. He ordered an American breakfast with scrambled eggs and sausage.

Ferris had come from Paris to his father's funeral

which had taken place the week before in his home town in Georgia. The shock of death had made him aware of youth already passed. His hair was receding and prominent and his body was spare except for an incipient belly bulge. Ferris had loved his father and the bond between them had once been extraordinarily close – but the years had somehow unravelled this filial devotion; the death, expected for a long time, had left him with an unforeseen dismay. He had stayed as long as possible to be near his mother and brothers at home. His plane for Paris was to leave the next morning.

Ferris pulled out his address book to verify a number. He turned the pages with growing attentiveness. Names and addresses from New York, the capitals of Europe, a few faint ones from his home state in the South. Faded, printed names, sprawled drunken ones. Betty Wills: a random love, married now. Charlie Williams: wounded in the Hürtgen Forest, unheard of since. Grand old Williams – did he live or die? Don Walker: a BTO in television, getting rich. Henry Green: hit the skids after the war, in a sanatorium now, they say. Cozie Hall: he had heard that she was dead. Heedless, laughing Cozie – it was strange to think that she too, silly girl, could die. As Ferris closed the address book, he suffered a sense of hazard, transience, almost of fear.

It was then that his body jerked suddenly. He was

staring out of the window when there, on the sidewalk, passing by, was his ex-wife. Elizabeth passed quite close to him, walking slowly. He could not understand the wild quiver of his heart, nor the following sense of recklessness and grace that lingered after she was gone.

Quickly Ferris paid his cheque and rushed out to the sidewalk. Elizabeth stood on the corner waiting to cross Fifth Avenue. He hurried towards her meaning to speak, but the lights changed and she crossed the street before he reached her. Ferris followed. On the other side he could easily have overtaken her, but he found himself lagging unaccountably. Her fair brown hair was plainly rolled, and as he watched her Ferris recalled that once his father had remarked that Elizabeth had a 'beautiful carriage'. She turned at the next corner and Ferris followed, although by now his intention to overtake her had disappeared. Ferris questioned the bodily disturbance that the sight of Elizabeth aroused in him, the dampness of his hands, the hard heart-strokes.

It was eight years since Ferris had last seen his ex-wife. He knew that long ago she had married again. And there were children. During recent years he had seldom thought of her. But at first, after the divorce, the loss had almost destroyed him. Then, after the anodyne of time, he had loved again, and then again. Jeannine, she was now. Certainly his love for his ex-wife was long since past. So why the unhinged body, the shaken mind? He knew only that his clouded heart was oddly dissonant with the sunny, candid autumn day. Ferris wheeled suddenly and, walking with long strides, almost running, hurried back to the hotel.

Ferris poured himself a drink, although it was not yet eleven o'clock. He sprawled out in an armchair like a man exhausted, nursing his glass of bourbon and water. He had a full day ahead of him as he was leaving by plane the next morning for Paris. He checked over his obligations: take luggage to Air France, lunch with his boss, buy shoes and an overcoat. And something – wasn't there something else? Ferris finished his drink and opened the telephone directory.

His decision to call his ex-wife was impulsive. The number was under Bailey, the husband's name, and he called before he had much time for self-debate. He and Elizabeth had exchanged cards at Christmas-time, and Ferris had sent a carving set when he received the announcement of her wedding. There was no reason *not* to call. But as he waited, listening to the ring at the other end, misgiving fretted him.

Elizabeth answered; her familiar voice was a fresh shock to him. Twice he had to repeat his name, but, when he was identified, she sounded glad. He explained he was only in town for that day. They had a theatre engagement, she said – but she wondered if he would come by for an early dinner. Ferris said he would be delighted.

As he went from one engagement to another, he was still bothered at odd moments by the feeling that something necessary was forgotten. Ferris bathed and changed in the late afternoon, often thinking about Jeannine: he would be with her the following night. 'Jeannine,' he would say, 'I happened to run into my ex-wife when I was in New York. Had dinner with her. And her husband, of course. It was strange seeing her after all these years.'

Elizabeth lived in the East Fifties, and as Ferris taxied uptown he glimpsed at intersections the lingering sunset, but by the time he reached his destination it was already autumn dark. The place was a building with a marquee and a doorman, and the apartment was on the seventh floor.

'Come in, Mr Ferris.'

Braced for Elizabeth or even the unimagined husband, Ferris was astonished by the freckled red-haired child; he had known of the children, but his mind had failed somehow to acknowledge them. Surprise made him step back awkwardly.

'This is our apartment,' the child said politely. 'Aren't you Mr Ferris? I'm Billy. Come in.'

In the living-room beyond the hall the husband

provided another surprise; he too had not been acknowledged emotionally. Bailey was a lumbering red-haired man with a deliberate manner. He rose and extended a welcoming hand.

'I'm Bill Bailey. Glad to see you. Elizabeth will be in in a minute. She's finishing dressing.'

The last words struck a gliding series of vibrations, memories of the other years. Fair Elizabeth, rosy and naked before her bath. Half-dressed before the mirror of her dressing-table, brushing her fine, chestnut hair. Sweet, casual intimacy, the soft-fleshed loveliness indisputably possessed. Ferris shrank from the unbidden memories and compelled himself to meet Bill Bailey's gaze.

'Billy, will you please bring that tray of drinks from the kitchen table?'

The child obeyed promptly, and when he was gone Ferris remarked conversationally, 'Fine boy you have there.'

'We think so.'

Flat silence until the child returned with a tray of glasses and a cocktail shaker of Martinis. With the priming drinks they pumped up conversation: Russia, they spoke of, and the New York rain-making, and the apartment situation in Manhattan and Paris.

'Mr Ferris is flying all the way across the ocean

tomorrow,' Bailey said to the little boy who was perched on the arm of his chair, quiet and well behaved. 'I bet you would like to be a stowaway in his suitcase.'

Billy pushed back his limp bangs. 'I want to fly in an aeroplane and be a newspaperman like Mr Ferris.' He added with sudden assurance, 'That's what I would like to do when I am big.'

Bailey said, 'I thought you wanted to be a doctor.'

'I do!' said Billy. 'I would like to be both. I want to be an atom-bomb scientist too.'

Elizabeth came in carrying in her arms a baby girl.

'Oh, John!' she said. She settled the baby in the father's lap. 'It's grand to see you. I'm awfully glad you could come.'

The little girl sat demurely on Bailey's knees. She wore a pale pink *crêpe-de-Chine* frock, smocked around the yoke with rose, and a matching silk hair ribbon tying back her pale soft curls. Her skin was summer tanned and her brown eyes flecked with gold and laughing. When she reached up and fingered her father's horn-rimmed glasses, he took them off and let her look through them a moment. 'How's my old Candy?'

Elizabeth was very beautiful, more beautiful perhaps than he had ever realized. Her straight clean hair was shining. Her face was softer, glowing and serene. It was a madonna loveliness, dependent on the family ambience.

'You've hardly changed at all,' Elizabeth said, 'but it has been a long time.'

'Eight years.' His hand touched his thinning hair self-consciously while further amenities were exchanged.

Ferris felt himself suddenly a spectator – an interloper among these Baileys. Why had he come? He suffered. His own life seemed so solitary, a fragile column supporting nothing amidst the wreckage of the years. He felt he could not bear much longer to stay in the family room.

He glanced at his watch. 'You're going to the theatre?'

'It's a shame,' Elizabeth said, 'but we've had this engagement for more than a month. But surely, John, you'll be staying home one of these days before long. You're not going to be an expatriate, are you?'

'Expatriate,' Ferris repeated. 'I don't much like the word.'

'What's a better word?' she asked.

He thought for a moment. 'Sojourner might do.'

Ferris glanced again at his watch, and again Elizabeth apologized. 'If only we had known ahead of time –'

'I just had this day in town. I came home unexpectedly. You see, Papa died last week.'

'Papa Ferris is dead?'

'Yes, at Johns-Hopkins. He had been sick there nearly a year. The funeral was down home in Georgia.'

'Oh, I'm so sorry, John. Papa Ferris was always one of my favourite people.'

The little boy moved from behind the chair so that he could look into his mother's face. He asked, 'Who is dead?'

Ferris was oblivious to apprehension; he was thinking of his father's death. He saw again the outstretched body on the quilted silk within the coffin. The corpse-flesh was bizarrely rouged and the familiar hands lay massive and joined above a spread of funeral roses. The memory closed and Ferris awakened to Elizabeth's calm voice.

'Mr Ferris's father, Billy. A really grand person. Somebody you didn't know.'

'But why did you call him *Papa* Ferris?'

Bailey and Elizabeth exchanged a trapped look. It was Bailey who answered the questioning child. 'A long time ago,' he said, 'your mother and Mr Ferris were once married. Before you were born – a long time ago.'

'Mr Ferris?'

The little boy stared at Ferris, amazed and unbelieving. And Ferris's eyes, as he returned the gaze, were somehow unbelieving too. Was it indeed true that at one time he had called this stranger Elizabeth, Little Butterduck during nights of love, that they had lived together, shared perhaps a thousand days and nights and – finally – endured in the misery of sudden solitude the fibre by fibre (jealousy, alcohol, and money quarrels) destruction of the fabric of married love.

Bailey said to the children, 'It's somebody's supper-time. Come on now.'

'But, Daddy! Mama and Mr Ferris – I –'

Billy's everlasting eyes – perplexed and with a glimmer of hostility – reminded Ferris of the gaze of another child. It was the young son of Jeannine – a boy of seven with a shadowed little face and nobbly knees whom Ferris avoided and usually forgot.

'Quick march!' Bailey gently turned Billy towards the door. 'Say good night now, son.'

'Good night, Mr Ferris.' He added resentfully, 'I thought I was staying up for the cake.'

'You can come in afterward for the cake,' Elizabeth said. 'Run along now with Daddy for your supper.'

Ferris and Elizabeth were alone. The weight of the situation descended on those first moments of silence. Ferris asked permission to pour himself another drink and Elizabeth set the cocktail shaker on the table at his side. He looked at the grand piano and noticed the music on the rack.

'Do you still play as beautifully as you used to?'

'I still enjoy it.'

'Please play, Elizabeth.'

Elizabeth arose immediately. Her readiness to perform

when asked had always been one of her amiabilities; she never hung back, apologized. Now as she approached the piano there was the added readiness of relief.

She began with a Bach prelude and fugue. The prelude was as gaily iridescent as a prism in a morning-room. The first voice of the fugue, an announcement pure and solitary, was repeated intermingling with a second voice, and again repeated within an elaborated frame, the multiple music, horizontal and serene, flowed with unhurried majesty. The principal melody was woven with two other voices, embellished with countless ingenuities – now dominant, again submerged, it had the sublimity of a single thing that does not fear surrender to the whole. Towards the end, the density of the material gathered for the last enriched insistence on the dominant first motif and with a chorded final statement the figure ended. Ferris rested his head on the chair back and closed his eyes. In the following silence a clear, high voice came from the room down the hall.

'Daddy, how *could* Mama and Mr Ferris –' A door was closed.

The piano began again – what was this music? Unplaced, familiar, the limpid melody had lain a long while dormant in his heart. Now it spoke to him of another time, another place – it was the music Elizabeth used to play. The delicate air summoned a wilderness of memory. Ferris was lost in the riot of past longings, conflicts, ambivalent desires. Strange that the music, catalyst for this tumultuous anarchy, was so serene and clear. The singing melody was broken off by the appearance of the maid.

'Miz Bailey, dinner is out on the table now.'

Even after Ferris was seated at the table between his host and hostess, the unfinished music still overcast his mood. He was a little drunk.

'*L'improvisation de la vie humaine*,' he said. 'There's nothing that makes you so aware of the improvisation of human existence as a song unfinished. Or an old address book.'

'Address book?' repeated Bailey. Then he stopped, non-committal and polite.

'You're still the same old boy, Johnny,' Elizabeth said with a trace of the old tenderness.

It was a Southern dinner that evening, and the dishes were his old favourites. They had fried chicken and corn pudding and rich, glazed candied sweet potatoes. During the meal Elizabeth kept alive a conversation when the silences were over-long. And it came about that Ferris was led to speak of Jeannine.

'I first knew Jeannine last autumn – about this time of the year – in Italy. She's a singer and she had an engagement in Rome. I expect we will be married soon.'

The words seemed so true, inevitable, that Ferris did not at first acknowledge to himself the lie. He and Jeannine had never in that year spoken of marriage. And indeed, she was still married – to a White Russian money-changer in Paris from whom she had been separated for five years. But it was too late to correct the lie. Already Elizabeth was saying: 'This really makes me glad to know. Congratulations, Johnny.'

He tried to make amends with truth. 'The Roman autumn is so beautiful. Balmy and blossoming.' He added, 'Jeannine has a little boy of six. A curious trilingual little fellow. We go to the Tuileries sometimes.'

A lie again. He had taken the boy once to the gardens. The sallow foreign child in shorts that bared his spindly legs had sailed his boat in the concrete pond and ridden the pony. The child had wanted to go in to the puppet show. But there was not time, for Ferris had an engagement at the Scribe Hotel. He had promised they would go to the guignol another afternoon. Only once had he taken Valentin to the Tuileries.

There was a stir. The maid brought in a white-frosted cake with pink candles. The children entered in their night clothes. Ferris still did not understand.

'Happy birthday, John,' Elizabeth said. 'Blow out the candles.'

Ferris recognized his birthday date. The candles blew

out lingeringly and there was the smell of burning wax. Ferris was thirty-eight years old. The veins in his temples darkened and pulsed visibly.

'It's time you started for the theatre.'

Ferris thanked Elizabeth for the birthday dinner and said the appropriate good-byes. The whole family saw him to the door.

A high, thin moon shone above the jagged, dark skyscrapers. The streets were windy, cold. Ferris hurried to Third Avenue and hailed a cab. He gazed at the nocturnal city with the deliberate attentiveness of departure and perhaps farewell. He was alone. He longed for flight-time and the coming journey.

The next day he looked down on the city from the air, burnished in sunlight, toylike, precise. Then America was left behind and there was only the Atlantic and the distant European shore. The ocean was milky pale and placid beneath the clouds. Ferris dozed most of the day. Towards dark he was thinking of Elizabeth and the visit of the previous evening. He thought of Elizabeth among her family with longing, gentle envy, and inexplicable regret. He sought the melody, the unfinished air, that had so moved him. The cadence, some unrelated tones, were all that remained; the melody itself evaded him. He had found instead the first voice of the fugue that Elizabeth had played – it came to him, inverted mockingly and in a minor key. Suspended above the ocean the anxieties of transience and solitude no longer troubled him and he thought of his father's death with equanimity. During the dinner hour the plane reached the shore of France.

At midnight Ferris was in a taxi crossing Paris. It was a clouded night and mist wreathed the lights of the Place de la Concorde. The midnight bistros gleamed on the wet pavements. As always after a transocean flight the change of continents was too sudden. New York at morning, this midnight Paris. Ferris glimpsed the disorder of his life: the succession of cities, of transitory loves; and time, the sinister glissando of the years, time always.

'*Vite! Vite!*' he called in terror. '*Dépêchez-vous.*'

Valentin opened the door to him. The little boy wore pyjamas and an outgrown red robe. His grey eyes were shadowed and, as Ferris passed into the flat, they flickered momentarily.

'*J'attends Maman.*'

Jeannine was singing in a night club. She would not be home before another hour. Valentin returned to a drawing, squatting with his crayons over the paper on the floor. Ferris looked down at the drawing – it was a banjo player with notes and wavy lines inside a comic-strip balloon.

'We will go again to the Tuileries.'

The child looked up and Ferris drew him closer to his knees. The melody, the unfinished music that Elizabeth had played, came to him suddenly. Unsought, the load of memory jettisoned – this time bringing only recognition and sudden joy.

'Monsieur Jean,' the child said, 'did you see him?'

Confused, Ferris thought only of another child – the freckled, family-loved boy. 'See who, Valentin?'

'Your dead papa in Georgia.' The child added, 'Was he okay?'

Ferris spoke with rapid urgency: 'We will go often to the Tuileries. Ride the pony and we will go into the guignol. We will see the puppet show and never be in a hurry any more.'

'Monsieur Jean,' Valentin said. 'The guignol is now closed.'

Again, the terror, the acknowledgement of wasted years and death. Valentin, responsive and confident, still nestled in his arms. His cheek touched the soft cheek and felt the brush of the delicate eyelashes. With inner desperation he pressed the child close – as though an emotion as protean as his love could dominate the pulse of time.

# *A Domestic Dilemma*

On Thursday Martin Meadows left the office early enough to make the first express bus home. It was the hour when the evening lilac glow was fading in the slushy streets, but by the time the bus had left the Midtown terminal the bright city night had come. On Thursdays the maid had a half-day off and Martin liked to get home as soon as possible, since for the past year his wife had not been – well. This Thursday he was very tired and, hoping that no regular commuter would single him out for conversation, he fastened his attention to the newspaper until the bus had crossed the George Washington Bridge. Once on 9-W Highway Martin always felt that the trip was half-way done, he breathed deeply, even in cold weather when only ribbons of draught cut through the smoky air of the bus, confident that he was breathing country air. It used to be that at this point he would relax and begin to think with pleasure of his home. But in this last year nearness brought only a sense of tension and he did not anticipate the journey's end.

This evening Martin kept his face close to the window and watched the barren fields and lonely lights of passing townships. There was a moon, pale on the dark earth, and areas of late, porous snow; to Martin the countryside seemed vast and somehow desolate that evening. He took his hat from the rack and put his folded newspaper in the pocket of his overcoat a few minutes before time to pull the cord.

The cottage was a block from the bus stop, near the river but not directly on the shore; from the living-room window you could look across the street and opposite yard and see the Hudson. The cottage was modern, almost too white and new on the narrow plot of yard. In summer the grass was soft and bright and Martin carefully tended a flower border and a rose trellis. But during the cold, fallow months the yard was bleak and the cottage seemed naked. Lights were on that evening in all the rooms in the little house and Martin hurried up the front walk. Before the steps he stopped to move a wagon out of the way.

The children were in the living-room, so intent on play that the opening of the front door was at first unnoticed. Martin stood looking at his safe, lovely children. They had opened the bottom drawer of the secretary and taken out the Christmas decorations. Andy had managed to plug in the Christmas tree lights and the green and red bulbs glowed with out-of-season festivity on the rug of the living-room. At the moment he was trying to trail the bright cord over Marianne's rocking horse. Marianne sat on the floor pulling off an angel's wings. The children wailed a startling welcome. Martin swung the fat little baby girl up to his shoulder and Andy threw himself against his father's legs.

'Daddy, Daddy, Daddy!'

Martin set down the little girl carefully and swung Andy a few times like a pendulum. Then he picked up the Christmas-tree cord.

'What's all this stuff doing out? Help me put it back in the drawer. You're not to fool with the light socket. Remember I told you that before. I mean it, Andy.'

The six-year-old child nodded and shut the secretary drawer. Martin stroked his fair soft hair and his hand lingered tenderly on the nape of the child's frail neck.

'Had supper yet, Bumpkin?'

'It hurt. The toast was hot.'

The baby girl stumbled on the rug and, after the first surprise of the fall, began to cry; Martin picked her up and carried her in his arms back to the kitchen.

'See, Daddy,' said Andy. 'The toast –'

Emily had laid the children's supper on the uncovered porcelain table. There were two plates with the remains of cream-of-wheat and eggs and silver mugs that had held milk. There was also a platter of cinnamon toast, untouched except for one toothmarked bite. Martin sniffed the bitten piece and nibbled gingerly. Then he put the toast into the garbage pail.

'Hoo – phui – What on earth!'

Emily had mistaken the tin of cayenne for the cinnamon.

'I like to have burnt up,' Andy said. 'Drank water and ran outdoors and opened my mouth. Marianne didn't eat none.'

'Any,' corrected Martin. He stood helpless, looking around the walls of the kitchen. 'Well, that's that, I guess,' he said finally. 'Where is your mother now?'

'She's up in you alls' room.'

Martin left the children in the kitchen and went up to his wife. Outside the door he waited for a moment to still his anger. He did not knock and once inside the room he closed the door behind him.

Emily sat in the rocking chair by the window of the pleasant room. She had been drinking something from a tumbler and as he entered she put the glass hurriedly on the floor behind the chair. In her attitude there was confusion and guilt which she tried to hide by a show of spurious vivacity.

'Oh, Marty! You home already? The time slipped up on me. I was just going down –' She lurched to him and her kiss was strong with sherry. When he stood unresponsive she stepped back a pace and giggled nervously.

'What's the matter with you? Standing there like a barber pole. Is anything wrong with you?'

'Wrong with *me*?' Martin bent over the rocking chair and picked up the tumbler from the floor. 'If you could only realize how sick I am – how bad it is for all of us.'

Emily spoke in a false, airy voice that had become too familiar to him. Often at such times she affected a slight English accent, copying perhaps some actress she admired. 'I haven't the vaguest idea what you mean. Unless you are referring to the glass I used for a spot of sherry. I had a finger of sherry – maybe two. But what is the crime in that, pray tell me? I'm quite all right. Quite all right.'

'So anyone can see.'

As she went into the bathroom Emily walked with careful gravity. She turned on the cold water and dashed some on her face with her cupped hands, then patted herself dry with the corner of a bath towel. Her face was delicately featured and young, unblemished.

'I was just going down to make dinner.' She tottered and balanced herself by holding to the door frame.

'I'll take care of dinner. You stay up here. I'll bring it up.'

'I'll do nothing of the sort. Why, whoever heard of such a thing?'

'Please,' Martin said.

'Leave me alone. I'm quite all right. I was just on the way down –'

'Mind what I say.'

'Mind your grandmother.'

She lurched towards the door, but Martin caught her by the arm. 'I don't want the children to see you in this condition. Be reasonable.'

'Condition!' Emily jerked her arm. Her voice rose angrily. 'Why, because I drink a couple of sherries in the afternoon you're trying to make me out a drunkard. Condition! Why, I don't even touch whisky. As well you know. *I* don't swill liquor at bars. And that's more than you can say. I don't even have a cocktail at dinnertime. I only sometimes have a glass of sherry. What, I ask you, is the disgrace of that? Condition!'

Martin sought words to calm his wife. 'We'll have a quiet supper by ourselves up here. That's a good girl.' Emily sat on the side of the bed and he opened the door for a quick departure.

'I'll be back in a jiffy.'

As he busied himself with the dinner downstairs he was lost in the familiar question as to how this problem had come upon his home. He himself had always enjoyed a good drink. When they were still living in Alabama they had served long drinks or cocktails as a matter of course. For years they had drunk one or two – possibly three drinks before dinner, and at bedtime a long nightcap. Evenings before holidays they might get a buzz on, might even become a little tight. But alcohol had never seemed a problem to him, only a bothersome expense that with the increase in the family they could scarcely afford. It was only after his company had transferred him to New York that Martin was aware that certainly his wife was drinking too much. She was tippling, he noticed, during the day.

The problem acknowledged, he tried to analyse the source. The change from Alabama to New York had somehow disturbed her; accustomed to the idle warmth of a small Southern town, the matrix of the family and cousinship and childhood friends, she had failed to accommodate herself to the stricter, lonelier *mores* of the North. The duties of motherhood and housekeeping were onerous to her. Homesick for Paris City, she had made no friends in the suburban town. She read only magazines and murder books. Her interior life was insufficient without the artifice of alcohol.

The revelations of incontinence insidiously undermined his previous conceptions of his wife. There were times of unexplainable malevolence, times when the alcoholic fuse caused an explosion of unseemly anger. He encountered a latent coarseness in Emily, inconsistent with her natural simplicity. She lied about drinking and deceived him with unsuspected stratagems.

Then there was an accident. Coming home from work one evening about a year ago, he was greeted with screams from the children's room. He found Emily holding the baby, wet and naked from her bath. The baby had been dropped, her frail, frail skull striking the table edge, so that a thread of blood was soaking into the gossamer hair. Emily was sobbing and intoxicated. As Martin cradled the hurt child, so infinitely precious at that moment, he had an affrighted vision of the future.

The next day Marianne was all right. Emily vowed that never again would she touch liquor, and for a few weeks she was sober, cold, and downcast. Then gradually she began – not whisky or gin – but quantities of beer, or sherry, or outlandish liqueurs; once he had come across a hatbox of empty crème-de-menthe bottles. Martin found a dependable maid who managed the household competently. Virgie was also from Alabama and Martin had never dared tell Emily the wage-scale customary in New York. Emily's drinking was entirely secret now, done before he reached the house. Usually the effects were almost imperceptible – a looseness of movement or the heavy-lidded eyes. The times of irresponsibilities, such as the cayenne-pepper toast were rare, and Martin could dismiss his worries when Virgie was at the house. But, nevertheless, anxiety was always latent, a threat of indefined disaster that underlaid his days.

'Marianne!' Martin called, for even the recollection of that time brought the need for reassurance. The baby girl, no longer hurt, but no less precious to her father, came into the kitchen with her brother. Martin went on with the preparations for the meal. He opened a can of soup and put two chops in the frying-pan. Then he sat down by the table and took his Marianne on his knees for a pony ride. Andy watched them, his fingers wobbling the tooth that had been loose all that week.

'Andy-the-candyman!' Martin said. 'Is that old critter still in your mouth? Come closer, let Daddy have a look.'

'I got a string to pull it with.' The child brought from his pocket a tangled thread. 'Virgie said to tie it to the tooth and tie the other end to the doorknob and shut the door real suddenly.'

Martin took out a clean handkerchief and felt the loose tooth carefully. 'That tooth is coming out of my Andy's mouth tonight. Otherwise I'm awfully afraid we'll have a tooth tree in the family.'

'A what?'

'A tooth tree,' Martin said. 'You'll bite into something and swallow that tooth. And the tooth will take root in poor Andy's stomach and grow into a tooth tree with sharp little teeth instead of leaves.'

'Shoo, Daddy,' Andy said. But he held the tooth firmly between his grimy little thumb and forefinger. 'There ain't any tree like that. I never seen one.'

'There *isn't* any tree like that and I never *saw* one.'

Martin tensed suddenly. Emily was coming down the stairs. He listened to her fumbling footsteps, his arm embracing the little boy with dread. When Emily came into the room he saw from her movements and her sullen face that she had again been at the sherry bottle. She began to yank open drawers and set the table.

'Condition!' she said in a furry voice. 'You talk to me like that. Don't think I'll forget. I remember every dirty lie you say to me. Don't you think for a minute that I forget.'

'Emily!' he begged. 'The children –'

'The children – yes! Don't think I don't see through your dirty plots and schemes. Down here trying to turn my own children against me. Don't think I don't see and understand.'

'Emily! I beg you – please go upstairs.'

'So you can turn my children – my very own children –' Two large tears coursed rapidly down her cheeks. 'Trying to turn my little boy, my Andy, against his own mother.'

With drunken impulsiveness Emily knelt on the floor before the startled child. Her hands on his shoulders balanced her. 'Listen, my Andy – you wouldn't listen to any lies your father tells you? You wouldn't believe what he says? Listen, Andy, what was your father telling you before I came downstairs?' Uncertain, the child sought his father's face. 'Tell me. Mama wants to know.'

'About the tooth tree.'

'What?'

The child repeated the words and she echoed them with unbelieving terror. 'The tooth tree!' She swayed and renewed her grasp on the child's shoulder. 'I don't know what you're talking about. But listen, Andy, Mama is all right, isn't she?' The tears were spilling down her face and Andy drew back from her, for he was afraid. Grasping the table edge, Emily stood up.

'See! You have turned my child against me.'

Marianne began to cry, and Martin took her in his arms.

'That's all right, you can take *your* child. You have always shown partiality from the very first. I don't mind, but at least you can leave me my little boy.'

Andy edged close to his father and touched his leg. 'Daddy,' he wailed.

Martin took the children to the foot of the stairs. 'Andy, you take up Marianne and Daddy will follow you in a minute.'

'But Mama?' the child asked, whispering.

'Mama will be all right. Don't worry.'

Emily was sobbing at the kitchen table, her face buried in the crook of her arm. Martin poured a cup of soup and set it before her. Her rasping sobs unnerved him; the vehemence of her emotion, irrespective of the source, touched in him a strain of tenderness. Unwillingly he laid his hand on her dark hair. 'Sit up and drink the soup.' Her face as she looked up at him was chastened and imploring. The boy's withdrawal or the touch of Martin's hand had turned the tenor of her mood.

'Ma-Martin,' she sobbed. 'I'm so ashamed.'

'Drink the soup.'

Obeying him, she drank between gasping breaths. After a second cup she allowed him to lead her up to their room. She was docile now and more restrained. He laid her nightgown on the bed and was about to leave the room when a fresh round of grief, the alcoholic tumult, came again.

'He turned away. My Andy looked at me and turned away.'

Impatience and fatigue hardened his voice, but he spoke warily. 'You forget that Andy is still a little child – he can't comprehend the meaning of such scenes.'

'Did I make a scene? Oh, Martin, did I make a scene before the children?'

Her horrified face touched and amused him against

his will. 'Forget it. Put on your nightgown and go to sleep.'

'My child turned away from me. Andy looked at his mother and turned away. The children –'

She was caught in the rhythmic sorrow of alcohol. Martin withdrew from the room saying: 'For God's sake go to sleep. The children will forget by tomorrow.'

As he said this he wondered if it was true. Would the scene glide so easily from memory – or would it root in the unconscious to fester in the after-years? Martin did not know, and the last alternative sickened him. He thought of Emily, foresaw the morning-after humiliation: the shards of memory, the lucidities that glared from the obliterating darkness of shame. She would call the New York office twice – possibly three or four times. Martin anticipated his own embarrassment, wondering if the others at the office could possibly suspect. He felt that his secretary had divined the trouble long ago and that she pitied him. He suffered a moment of rebellion against his fate; he hated his wife.

Once in the children's room he closed the door and felt secure for the first time that evening. Marianne fell down on the floor, picked herself up and calling: 'Daddy, watch me,' fell again, got up, and continued the falling-calling routine. Andy sat in the child's low chair, wobbling the tooth. Martin ran the water in the tub, washed his own hands in the lavatory, and called the boy into the bathroom.

'Let's have another look at that tooth.' Martin sat on the toilet, holding Andy between his knees. The child's mouth gaped and Martin grasped the tooth. A wobble, a quick twist and the nacreous milk tooth was free. Andy's face was for the moment split between terror, astonishment, and delight. He mouthed a swallow of water and spat into the lavatory.

'Look, Daddy! It's blood. Marianne!'

Martin loved to bath his children, loved inexpressibly the tender, naked bodies as they stood in the water so exposed. It was not fair of Emily to say that he showed partiality. As Martin soaped the delicate boy-body of his son he felt that further love would be impossible. Yet he admitted the difference in the quality of his emotions for the two children. His love for his daughter was graver, touched with a strain of melancholy, a gentleness that was akin to pain. His pet names for the little boy were the absurdities of daily inspiration – he called the little girl always Marianne, and his voice as he spoke it was a caress. Martin patted dry the fat baby stomach and the sweet little genital fold. The washed child faces were radiant as flower petals, equally loved.

'I'm putting the tooth under my pillow. I'm supposed to get a quarter.'

'What for?'

'*You* know, Daddy. Johnny got a quarter for his tooth.'

'Who put the quarter there?' asked Martin. 'I used to think the fairies left it in the night. It was a dime in my day, though.'

'That's what they say in kindergarten.'

'Who does put it there?'

'Your parents,' Andy said. 'You!'

Martin was pinning the cover on Marianne's bed. His daughter was already asleep. Scarcely breathing, Martin bent over and kissed her forehead, kissed again the tiny hand that lay palm-upward, flung in slumber beside her head.

'Good night, Andy-man.'

The answer was only a drowsy murmur. After a minute Martin took out his change and slid a quarter underneath the pillow. He left a night-light in the room.

As Martin prowled about the kitchen making a late meal, it occurred to him that the children had not once mentioned their mother or the scene that must have seemed to them incomprehensible. Absorbed in the instant – the tooth, the bath, the quarter – the fluid passage of child-time had borne these weightless episodes like leaves in the swift current of a shallow stream while the adult enigma was beached and forgotten on the shore. Martin thanked the Lord for that.

But his own anger, repressed and lurking, arose again. His youth was being frittered by a drunkard's waste, his very manhood subtly undermined. And the children, once the immunity of incomprehension passed – what would it be like in a year or so? With his elbows on the table he ate his food brutishly, untasting. There was no hiding the truth – soon there would be gossip in the office and in the town; his wife was a dissolute woman. Dissolute. And he and his children were bound to a future of degradation and slow ruin.

Martin pushed away from the table and stalked into the living-room. He followed the lines of a book with his eyes, but his mind conjured miserable images: he saw his children drowned in the river, his wife a disgrace on the public street. By bedtime the dull, hard anger was like a weight upon his chest and his feet dragged as he climbed the stairs.

The room was dark except for the shafting light from the half-opened bathroom door. Martin undressed quietly. Little by little, mysteriously, there came in him a change. His wife was asleep, her peaceful respirations sounding gently in the room. Her high-heeled shoes with the carelessly dropped stockings made to him a mute appeal. Her underclothes were flung in disorder on the chair. Martin picked up the girdle and the soft, silk brassière and stood for a moment with them in his hands. For the first time that evening he looked at his wife. His eyes rested on the sweet forehead, the arch of the fine brow. The brow had descended to Marianne, and the tilt at the end of the delicate nose. In his son he could trace the high cheekbones and pointed chin. Her body was full-bosomed, slender, and undulant. As Martin watched the tranquil slumber of his wife the ghost of the old anger vanished. All thoughts of blame or blemish were distant from him now. Martin put out the bathroom light and raised the window. Careful not to awaken Emily he slid into the bed. By moonlight he watched his wife for the last time. His hand sought the adjacent flesh and sorrow paralleled desire in the immense complexity of love.

1. MARTIN LUTHER KING, JR. · *Letter from Birmingham Jail*
2. ALLEN GINSBERG · *Television Was a Baby Crawling Toward That Deathchamber*
3. DAPHNE DU MAURIER · *The Breakthrough*
4. DOROTHY PARKER · *The Custard Heart*
5. *Three Japanese Short Stories*
6. ANAÏS NIN · *The Veiled Woman*
7. GEORGE ORWELL · *Notes on Nationalism*
8. GERTRUDE STEIN · *Food*
9. STANISLAW LEM · *The Three Electroknights*
10. PATRICK KAVANAGH · *The Great Hunger*
11. DANILO KIŠ · *The Legend of the Sleepers*
12. RALPH ELLISON · *The Black Ball*
13. JEAN RHYS · *Till September Petronella*
14. FRANZ KAFKA · *Investigations of a Dog*
15. CLARICE LISPECTOR · *Daydream and Drunkenness of a Young Lady*
16. RYSZARD KAPUŚCIŃSKI · *An Advertisement for Toothpaste*
17. ALBERT CAMUS · *Create Dangerously*
18. JOHN STEINBECK · *The Vigilante*
19. FERNANDO PESSOA · *I Have More Souls Than One*
20. SHIRLEY JACKSON · *The Missing Girl*
21. *Four Russian Short Stories*
22. ITALO CALVINO · *The Distance of the Moon*
23. AUDRE LORDE · *The Master's Tools Will Never Dismantle the Master's House*
24. LEONORA CARRINGTON · *The Skeleton's Holiday*
25. WILLIAM S. BURROUGHS · *The Finger*

26. SAMUEL BECKETT · *The End*
27. KATHY ACKER · *New York City in 1979*
28. CHINUA ACHEBE · *Africa's Tarnished Name*
29. SUSAN SONTAG · *Notes on 'Camp'*
30. JOHN BERGER · *The Red Tenda of Bologna*
31. FRANÇOISE SAGAN · *The Gigolo*
32. CYPRIAN EKWENSI · *Glittering City*
33. JACK KEROUAC · *Piers of the Homeless Night*
34. HANS FALLADA · *Why Do You Wear a Cheap Watch?*
35. TRUMAN CAPOTE · *The Duke in His Domain*
36. SAUL BELLOW · *Leaving the Yellow House*
37. KATHERINE ANNE PORTER · *The Cracked Looking-Glass*
38. JAMES BALDWIN · *Dark Days*
39. GEORGES SIMENON · *Letter to My Mother*
40. WILLIAM CARLOS WILLIAMS · *Death the Barber*
41. BETTY FRIEDAN · *The Problem that Has No Name*
42. FEDERICO GARCÍA LORCA · *The Dialogue of Two Snails*
43. YUKO TSUSHIMA · *Of Dogs and Walls*
44. JAVIER MARÍAS · *Madame du Deffand and the Idiots*
45. CARSON MCCULLERS · *The Haunted Boy*
46. JORGE LUIS BORGES · *The Garden of Forking Paths*
47. ANDY WARHOL · *Fame*
48. PRIMO LEVI · *The Survivor*
49. VLADIMIR NABOKOV · *Lance*
50. WENDELL BERRY · *Why I Am Not Going to Buy a Computer*